THE CAT WHO LOVED TO SING

THE CAT WHO LOVED TO SING

By Nonny Hogrogian

ALFRED A. KNOPF NEW YORK

THIS IS A BORZOI BOOK PUBLISHED BY ALFRED A. KNOPF, INC.

 Published in the United States by Alfred A. Knopf, Inc., New York, and simultaneously in Canada by Random House of Canada Limited, Toronto. Distributed by Random House, Inc., New York.
Manufactured in the United States of America
1 3 5 7 9 0 8 6 4 2

Library of Congress Cataloging-in-Publication Data
Hogrogian, Nonny. The cat who loved to sing.
Summary: A cat who loves to sing trades one thing for another until he finally gains a mandolin.
[1. Cats—Fiction] I. Title.
PZ7.H6844Cat 1988 [E] 86-27358
ISBN 0-394-89004-3 ISBN 0-394-99004-8 (lib. bdg.)

FOR MICHAEL HEDGE WHO LOVES TO FISH

There once was a cat who loved to sing,
trala lala lala.

One day he was singing along
as he romped down a wooded path,
and suddenly he stepped on a thorn.
"Ow! Ow ow ow ow ow!" he cried,
and hopped along in pain.
"What ails you, poor cat?"
called a woman from her garden.
She put down her basket
and pulled out the thorn and said,
"What a fine needle this would make."

So she offered the cat some freshly baked bread
in return for the useful thorn.
"I gladly accept," said the cat,
"and thank you for your help."
And he went on his way down the wooded path
with the bread tucked under his arm.

Trala lala
I gave my thorn and got some bread
that I will eat with a succulent mouse.
Trala lala lala

A fox was running through the woods
with a hen he had snatched from a neighboring farm.
When he noticed the cat and smelled the fine loaf,
a thought came into his head.
"Think of *all* the fat chickens
I could lure with that bread—
certainly more than this one lonely hen."

So the fox jumped out and blocked the way
and offered the hen in return for the bread.

The cat gave up the bread
and accepted the hen
and continued on his way.

Trala lala
I gave my thorn and got some bread.
I lost the bread and gained a hen.
How tasty it will be.
Trala

The cat traveled on and he met a young bride.
"What a wonderful hen
you are holding," she said.
"It would make a fine treat for my husband's supper.
Will you trade it for some nice red yarn?"
"Yes, of course," said the cat.
And he gave the hen to the bride
in return for her yarn.

Trala lala
I gave my thorn and got some bread.
I lost the bread and gained a hen.
I gave the hen for some nice red yarn.
Trala lala lala

Just then an old woman came hobbling by.
"How lucky I am," she said.
"I was going to town to buy some yarn,
but I see that you have the perfect color.
Won't you accept this fine old coat
in exchange for that beautiful yarn?"
The cat agreed to the trade
and continued on his way.

Trala lala
I gave my thorn and got some bread.
I lost the bread and gained a hen.
I gave the hen for some nice red yarn.
I traded the yarn for a fine old coat.
Trala lala lala

He passed an old man in need of a coat.
"You may have my dog," the old man said,
"since I can hardly feed myself."
"A dog!" exclaimed the cat.
"I never dreamed of owning a dog!
But I haven't made a bad trade yet.
Yes, I will take your dog."
And he continued down the path.

Trala lala
I gave my thorn and got some bread.
I lost the bread and gained a hen.
I gave the hen for some nice red yarn.
I traded the yarn for a fine old coat.
I gave the coat for this scruffy dog.
Trala lala lala

He soon met a fellow who was taking a fat lamb to market. When the man saw the dog, he began to weep.

“Oh, he reminds me of my dog
who was lost so long ago,”
said the fellow.
“Would you take this fine lamb for the dog?”
“Of course,” said the cat,
and he continued on his way.

Trala lala
I gave my thorn and got some bread.
I lost the bread and gained a hen.
I gave the hen for some nice red yarn.
I traded the yarn for a fine old coat.
I gave the coat to get a dog.
I swapped the dog for a big fat lamb.
Trala

He then saw a sad shepherd by the side of the road
with a staff in one hand and a mandolin over his shoulder.
"What is wrong, my good fellow?" asked the cat.
"Why are you so sad?
With a mandolin like that
you can play music all the long day."

"But that is exactly how I lost my flock,"
said the shepherd.
"And what will I do now?"

"Well," said the cat,
"I have a nice fat lamb with
which you can start again."

The shepherd looked at the lamb
and clapped his hands in delight.
"Your nice fat lamb is about
to have more lambs," he said.
"That won't make a flock,
but it would be a start.
What can I give you in return?"
"I would love to have your mandolin," said the cat,
"for I am a cat who loves to sing."

And so they made the trade and the cat traveled on, strumming his new mandolin.

Trala lala
I gave my thorn and got some bread.
I lost the bread and gained a hen.
I gave the hen for some nice red yarn.
I traded the yarn for a fine old coat.
I gave the coat to get a dog
and swapped the dog for a nice fat lamb.
I traded the lamb for a mandolin,
and this I will keep to play my songs.
Trala lala lala lala.

The Butterfly that Stamped

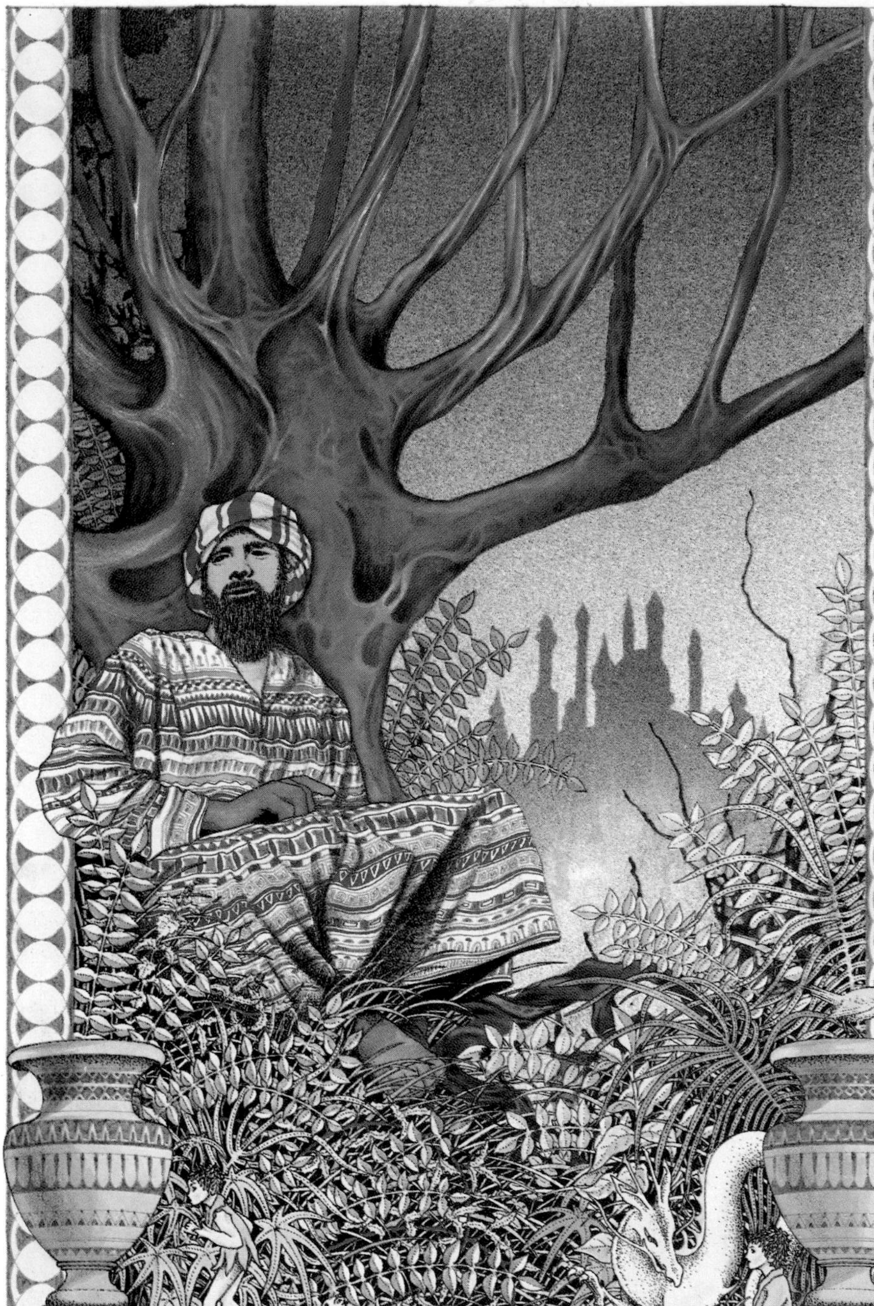

The Butterfly that Stamped

Rudyard Kipling
Illustrated by Alan Baker

PETER BEDRICK BOOKS
NEW YORK

First American edition published in 1983 by Peter Bedrick Books, 239 Central Park West, New York, N.Y. 10024. Published by agreement with Macmillan Children's Books, a division of Macmillan Publishers Ltd, London and Basingstoke.

ISBN 0-911745-04-1
LC 83-71482
Printed in Italy by
New Interlitho, Milan

Distributed in the USA by Harper & Row

THIS, O my Best Beloved, is a story—a new and a wonderful story—a story quite different from the other stories—a story about The Most Wise Sovereign Suleiman-bin-Daoud—Solomon the Son of David.

There are three hundred and fifty-five stories about Suleiman-bin-Daoud; but this is not one of them. It is not the story of the Lapwing who found the Water; or the Hoopoe who shaded Suleiman-bin-Daoud from the heat. It is not the story of the Glass Pavement, or the Ruby with the Crooked Hole, or the Gold Bars of Balkis. It is the story of the Butterfly that Stamped.

Now attend all over again and listen!

Suleiman-bin-Daoud was wise. He understood what the beasts said, what the birds said, what the fishes said, and what the insects said. He understood what the rocks said deep under the earth when they bowed in towards each other and groaned; and he understood what the trees said when they rustled in the middle of the morning. He understood everything, from the bishop on the bench to the hyssop on the wall; and Balkis, his Head Queen, the Most Beautiful Queen Balkis, was nearly as wise as he was.

Suleiman-bin-Daoud was strong. Upon the third finger of his right hand he wore a ring. When he turned it once, Afrits and Djinns came out of the earth to do whatever he told them. When he turned it twice, Fairies came down from the sky to do whatever he told them; and when he turned it three times, the very great angel

Azrael of the Sword came dressed as a water-carrier, and told him the news of the three worlds,—Above—Below—and Here.

And yet Suleiman-bin-Daoud was not proud. He very seldom showed off, and when he did he was sorry for it. Once he tried to feed all the animals in all the world in one day, but when the food was ready an Animal came out of the deep sea and ate it up in three mouthfuls. Suleiman-bin-Daoud was very surprised and said, 'O Animal, who are you?' And the Animal said, 'O King, live for ever! I am the smallest of thirty thousand brothers, and our home is at the bottom of the sea. We heard that you were going to feed all the animals in all the world, and my brothers sent me to ask when dinner would be ready.' Suleiman-bin-Daoud was more surprised than ever and said, 'O Animal, you have eaten all the dinner that I made ready for all the animals in the world.' And the Animal said, 'O King, live for ever, but do you really call *that* a dinner? Where I come from we each eat twice as much as that between meals.' Then Suleiman-bin-Daoud fell flat on his face and said, 'O Animal! I gave that dinner to show what a great and rich king I was, and not because I really wanted to be kind to the animals. Now I am ashamed, and it serves me right.' Suleiman-bin-Daoud was a really truly wise man, Best Beloved. After that he never forgot that it was silly to show off; and now the real story part of my story begins.

He married ever so many wives. He married nine hundred and ninety-nine wives, besides the Most

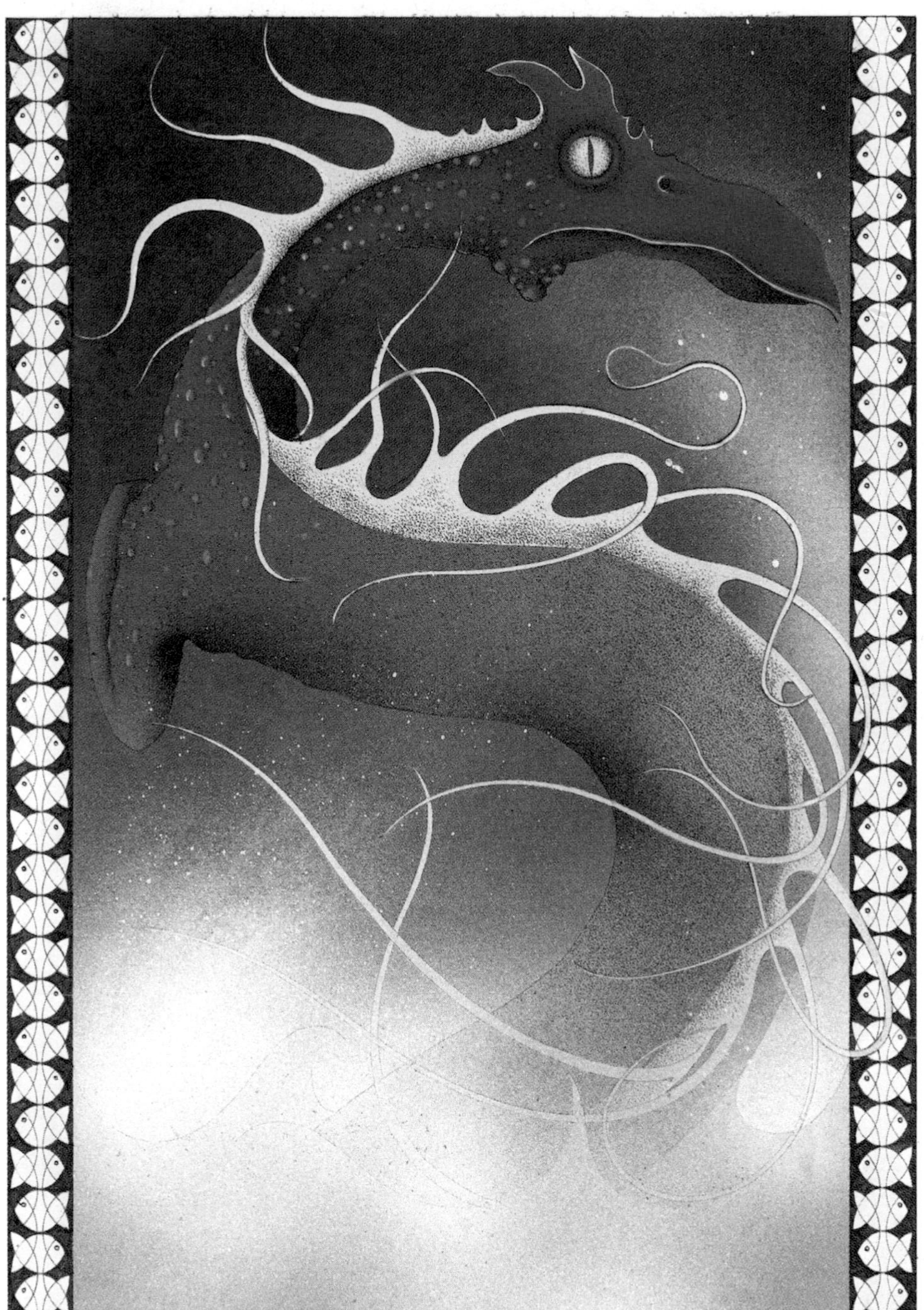

Beautiful Balkis; and they all lived in a great golden palace in the middle of a lovely garden with fountains. He didn't really want nine hundred and ninety-nine wives, but in those days everybody married ever so many wives, and of course the King had to marry ever so many more just to show that he was the King.

Some of the wives were nice, but some were simply horrid, and the horrid ones quarrelled with the nice ones and made them horrid too, and then they would all quarrel with Suleiman-bin-Daoud, and that was horrid for him. But Balkis the Most Beautiful never quarrelled with Suleiman-bin-Daoud. She loved him too much. She sat in her rooms in the Golden Palace, or walked in the Palace garden, and was truly sorry for him.

Of course if he had chosen to turn his ring on his finger and call up the Djinns and the Afrits they would have magicked all those nine hundred and ninety-nine quarrelsome wives into white mules of the desert or greyhounds or pomegranate seeds; but Suleiman-bin-Daoud thought that that would be showing off. So, when they quarrelled too much, he only walked by himself in one part of the beautiful Palace gardens and wished he had never been born.

One day, when they had quarrelled for three weeks—all nine hundred and ninety-nine wives together—Suleiman-bin-Daoud went out for peace and quiet as usual; and among the orange-trees he met Balkis the Most Beautiful, very sorrowful because Suleiman-bin-Daoud was so worried. And she said to him, 'O my Lord and Light of my Eyes, turn the ring upon your finger and show these Queens of Egypt and Mesopotamia and Persia and China that you are the great and terrible King.' But Suleiman-bin-Daoud shook his head and said, 'O my Lady and Delight of my Life, remember the Animal that came out of the sea and made me ashamed before all the animals in all the world because I showed off. Now, if I showed off before these Queens of Persia and Egypt and Abyssinia and China, merely because they worry me, I might be made even more ashamed than I have been.'

And Balkis the Most Beautiful said, 'O my Lord and Treasure of my Soul, what will you do?'

And Suleiman-bin-Daoud said, 'O my Lady and Content of my Heart, I shall continue to endure my fate at the hands of these nine hundred and ninety-nine Queens who vex me with their continual quarrelling.'

So he went on between the lilies and the loquats and the roses and the cannas and the heavy-scented ginger-plants that grew in the garden, till he came to the great camphor-tree that was called the Camphor-Tree of Suleiman-bin-Daoud. But Balkis hid among the tall irises and the spotted bamboos and the red lilies behind the camphor-tree, so as to be near her own true love, Suleiman-bin-Daoud.

Presently two Butterflies flew under the tree, quarrelling.

Suleiman-bin-Daoud heard one say to the other, 'I wonder at your presumption in talking like this to me.

Don't you know that if I stamped with my foot all Suleiman-bin-Daoud's Palace and this garden here would immediately vanish in a clap of thunder?'

Then Suleiman-bin-Daoud forgot his nine hundred and ninety-nine bothersome wives, and laughed, till the camphor-tree shook, at the Butterfly's boast. And he held out his finger and said, 'Little man, come here.'

The Butterfly was dreadfully frightened, but he managed to fly up to the hand of Suleiman-bin-Daoud, and clung there, fanning himself. Suleiman-bin-Daoud bent his head and whispered very softly, 'Little man, you know that all your stamping wouldn't bend one blade of grass. What made you tell that awful fib to your wife?—for doubtless she is your wife.'

The Butterfly looked at Suleiman-bin-Daoud and saw the most wise King's eyes twinkle like stars on a frosty night, and he picked up his courage with both wings, and he put his head on one side and said, 'O King, live for ever! She *is* my wife; and you know what wives are like.'

Suleiman-bin-Daoud smiled in his beard and said, 'Yes, *I* know, little brother.'

'One must keep them in order somehow,' said the Butterfly, 'and she has been quarrelling with me all the morning. I said that to quiet her.'

And Suleiman-bin-Daoud said, 'May it quiet her. Go back to your wife, little brother, and let me hear what you say.'

Back flew the Butterfly to his wife, who was all of a

twitter behind a leaf, and she said, 'He heard you! Suleiman-bin-Daoud himself heard you!'

'Heard me!' said the Butterfly. 'Of course he did. I meant him to hear me.'

'And what did he say? Oh, what did he say?'

'Well,' said the Butterfly, fanning himself most importantly, 'between you and me, my dear—of course I don't blame him, because his Palace must have cost a great deal and the oranges are just ripening,—he asked me not to stamp, and I promised I wouldn't.'

'Gracious!' said his wife, and sat quite quiet; but Suleiman-bin-Daoud laughed till the tears ran down his face at the impudence of the bad little Butterfly.

Balkis the Most Beautiful stood up behind the tree among the red lilies and smiled to herself, for she had heard all this talk. She thought, 'If I am wise I can yet save my Lord from the persecutions of these quarrelsome Queens,' and she held out her finger and whispered softly to the Butterfly's Wife, 'Little woman, come here.'

Up flew the Butterfly's Wife, very frightened, and clung to Balkis's white hand.

Balkis bent her beautiful head down and whispered, 'Little woman, do you believe what your husband has just said?'

The Butterfly's Wife looked at Balkis, and saw the Most Beautiful Queen's eyes shining like deep pools with starlight on them, and she picked up her courage with both wings and said, 'O Queen, be lovely for ever!

You know what men-folk are like.'

And the Queen Balkis, the Wise Balkis of Sheba, put her hand to her lips to hide a smile, and said, 'Little sister, *I* know.'

'They get angry,' said the Butterfly's Wife, fanning herself quickly, 'over nothing at all, but we must humour them, O Queen. They never mean half they say. If it pleases my husband to believe that I believe he can make Suleiman-bin-Daoud's Palace disappear by stamping his foot, I'm sure *I* don't care. He'll forget all about it to-morrow.'

'Little sister,' said Balkis, 'you are quite right; but next time he begins to boast, take him at his word. Ask him to stamp, and see what will happen. *We* know what men-folk are like, don't we? He'll be very much ashamed.'

Away flew the Butterfly's Wife to her husband, and in five minutes they were quarrelling worse than ever.

'Remember!' said the Butterfly. 'Remember what I can do if I stamp my foot.'

'I don't believe you one little bit,' said the Butterfly's Wife. 'I should very much like to see it done. Suppose you stamp now.'

'I promised Suleiman-bin-Daoud that I wouldn't,' said the Butterfly, 'and I don't want to break my promise.'

'It wouldn't matter if you did,' said his wife. 'You couldn't bend a blade of grass with your stamping. I dare you to do it,' she said. 'Stamp! Stamp! Stamp!'

Suleiman-bin-Daoud, sitting under the camphor-tree,

heard every word of this, and he laughed as he had never laughed in his life before. He forgot all about his Queens; he forgot about the Animal that came out of the sea; he forgot about showing off. He just laughed with joy, and Balkis, on the other side of the tree, smiled because her own true love was so joyful.

Presently the Butterfly, very hot and puffy, came whirling back under the shadow of the camphor-tree and said to Suleiman, 'She wants me to stamp! She wants to see what will happen, O Suleiman-bin-Daoud! You know I can't do it, and now she'll never believe a word I say. She'll laugh at me to the end of my days!'

'No, little brother,' said Suleiman-bin-Daoud, 'she will never laugh at you again,' and he turned the ring on his finger—just for the little Butterfly's sake, not for the sake of showing off,—and, lo and behold, four huge Djinns came out of the earth!

'Slaves,' said Suleiman-bin-Daoud, 'when this gentleman on my finger' (that was where the impudent Butterfly was sitting) 'stamps his left front forefoot you will make my Palace and these gardens disappear in a clap of thunder. When he stamps again you will bring them back carefully.'

'Now, little brother,' he said, 'go back to your wife and stamp all you've a mind to.'

Away flew the Butterfly to his wife, who was crying, 'I dare you to do it! I dare you to do it! Stamp! Stamp now! Stamp!' Balkis saw the four vast Djinns stoop down to the four corners of the gardens with the Palace in the

middle, and she clapped her hands softly and said, 'At last Suleiman-bin-Daoud will do for the sake of a Butterfly what he ought to have done long ago for his own sake, and the quarrelsome Queens will be frightened!'

Then the Butterfly stamped. The Djinns jerked the Palace and the gardens a thousand miles into the air: there was a most awful thunder-clap, and everything grew inky black. The Butterfly's Wife fluttered about in the dark, crying, 'Oh, I'll be good! I'm so sorry I spoke! Only bring the gardens back, my dear darling husband, and I'll never contradict again.'

The Butterfly was nearly as frightened as his wife, and Suleiman-bin-Daoud laughed so much that it was several minutes before he found breath enough to whisper to the Butterfly, 'Stamp again, little brother. Give me back my Palace, most great magician.'

'Yes, give him back his Palace,' said the Butterfly's Wife, still flying about in the dark like a moth. 'Give him back his Palace, and don't let's have any more horrid magic.'

'Well, my dear,' said the Butterfly as bravely as he could, 'you see what your nagging has led to. Of course it doesn't make any difference to *me*—I'm used to this kind of thing—but as a favour to you and to Suleiman-bin-Daoud I don't mind putting things right.'

So he stamped once more, and that instant the Djinns let down the Palace and the gardens, without even a bump. The sun shone on the dark-green orange-leaves; the fountains played among the pink Egyptian lilies; the birds went on singing; and the Butterfly's Wife lay on her side under the camphor-tree waggling her wings and panting, 'Oh, I'll be good! I'll be good!'

Suleiman-bin-Daoud could hardly speak for laughing. He leaned back all weak and hiccoughy, and shook his finger at the Butterfly and said, 'O great wizard, what is the sense of returning to me my Palace if at the same time you slay me with mirth?'

Then came a terrible noise, for all the nine hundred and ninety-nine Queens ran out of the Palace shrieking and shouting and calling for their babies. They hurried down the great marble steps below the fountain, one hundred abreast, and the Most Wise Balkis went statelily forward to meet them and said, 'What is your trouble, O Queens?'

They stood on the marble steps one hundred abreast and shouted, '*What* is our trouble? We were living peacefully in our golden Palace, as is our custom, when upon a sudden the Palace disappeared, and we were left sitting in a thick and noisome darkness; and it thundered, and Djinns and Afrits moved about in the darkness! *That* is our trouble, O Head Queen, and we are most extremely troubled on account of that trouble, for it was a troublesome trouble, unlike any trouble we have known.'

Then Balkis the Most Beautiful Queen—Suleiman-bin-Daoud's Very Best Beloved—Queen that was of Sheba and Sabie and the Rivers of the Gold of the South—from the Desert of Zinn to the Towers of

Zimbabwe—Balkis, almost as wise as the Most Wise Suleiman-bin-Daoud himself, said, 'It is nothing, O Queens! A Butterfly has made complaint against his wife because she quarrelled with him, and it has pleased our Lord Suleiman-bin-Daoud to teach her a lesson in low-speaking and humbleness, for that is counted a virtue among the wives of the butterflies.'

Then up and spoke an Egyptian Queen—the daughter of a Pharaoh—and she said, 'Our Palace cannot be plucked up by the roots like a leek for the sake of a little insect. No! Suleiman-bin-Daoud must be dead, and what we heard and saw was the earth thundering and darkening at the news.'

Then Balkis beckoned that bold Queen without looking at her, and said to her and to the others, 'Come and see.'

They came down the marble steps, one hundred abreast, and beneath his camphor-tree, still weak with laughing, they saw the Most Wise King Suleiman-bin-Daoud rocking back and forth with a Butterfly on either hand, and they heard him say, 'O wife of my brother in the air, remember after this to please your husband in all things, lest he be provoked to stamp his foot yet again; for he has said that he is used to this Magic, and he is most eminently a great magician—one who steals away the very Palace of Suleiman-bin-Daoud himself. Go in peace, little folk!' And he kissed them on the wings, and they flew away.

Then all the Queens except Balkis—the Most Beautiful

and Splendid Balkis, who stood apart smiling—fell flat on their faces, for they said, 'If these things are done when a Butterfly is displeased with his wife, what shall be done to us who have vexed our King with our loud-speaking and open quarrelling through many days?'

Then they put their veils over their heads, and they put their hands over their mouths, and they tiptoed back to the Palace most mousy-quiet.

Then Balkis—the Most Beautiful and Excellent Balkis—went forward through the red lilies into the shade of the camphor-tree and laid her hand upon Suleiman-bin-Daoud's shoulder and said, 'O my Lord and Treasure of my Soul, rejoice, for we have taught the Queens of Egypt and Mesopotamia and Abyssinia and Persia and India and China with a great and a memorable teaching.'

And Suleiman-bin-Daoud, still looking after the Butterflies where they played in the sunlight, said, 'O my Lady and Jewel of my Felicity, when did this happen? For I have been jesting with a Butterfly ever since I came into the garden.' And he told Balkis what he had done.

Balkis—the Tender and Most Lovely Balkis—said, 'O my Lord and Regent of my Existence, I hid behind the camphor-tree and saw it all. It was I who told the Butterfly's Wife to ask the Butterfly to stamp, because I hoped that for the sake of the jest my Lord would make some great Magic and that the Queens would see it and be frightened.' And she told him what the Queens had said and seen and thought.

Then Suleiman-bin-Daoud rose up from his seat under the camphor-tree, and stretched his arms and rejoiced and said, 'O my Lady and Sweetener of my Days, know that if I had made a Magic against my Queens for the sake of pride or anger, as I made that feast for all the animals, I should certainly have been put to shame. But by means of your wisdom I made the Magic for the sake of a jest and for the sake of a little Butterfly, and—behold—it has also delivered me from the vexations of my vexatious wives! Tell me, therefore, O my Lady and Heart of my Heart, how did you come to be so wise?'

And Balkis the Queen, beautiful and tall, looked up into Suleiman-bin-Daoud's eyes and put her head a little on one side, just like the Butterfly, and said, 'First, O my Lord, because I loved you; and secondly, O my Lord, because I know what women-folk are.'

Then they went up to the Palace and lived happily ever afterwards.

But wasn't it clever of Balkis?

There was never a Queen like Balkis,
From here to the wide world's end;
But Balkis talked to a butterfly
As you would talk to a friend.

There was never a King like Solomon,
Not since the world began;
But Solomon talked to a butterfly
As a man would talk to a man.

She was Queen of Sabaea—
And he was Asia's Lord—
But they both of 'em talked to butterflies
When they took their walks abroad!